SCOT GARDNER

DARK STONE EYE

SCOT GARDNER

DARK STONE EYE

www.pearsoned.co.nz

Your comments on this title are welcome at
feedback@pearsoned.co.nz

Pearson
a division of Pearson New Zealand Ltd
67 Apollo Drive, Rosedale, Auckland 0632, New Zealand

Associated companies throughout the world

Dark Stone Eye

Story by Scot Gardner

U.S. edition by Houghton Mifflin Harcourt Publishing Company

Printed in China via Pearson Education Asia (EPC/01)

ISBN 978-0-5479-8600-5

10 9 8 7 6   1846   12 11 10
4500000000   A B C D E F G

AUTHOR'S NOTE

My life is layers and layers of stories. My bones, like your bones, probably contain elements (like carbon and calcium) that have been in use since the dawn of time. Tiny parts of you were roaming the Earth as dinosaurs and probably traveled through space as space dust. Imagine if you could remember all those stories? Wouldn't that blow your mind?

Scot Gardner

For Robyn, who gives me lots of things,
including the idea for this book.

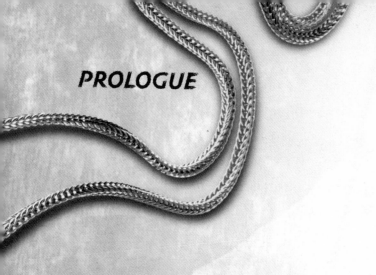

PROLOGUE

Every single thing in the whole wide world has a story. Everything. Every grain of sand was once part of a rock born in the steaming guts of the Earth. That's a story—a big story. Even the school computer I'm typing this story on is full of stories. Metal from the beginning of the universe (so Mr. Jensen says), melted sand (for the glass screen), and plastic. Don't get Mr. Jensen started on the story of plastic. It's made from oil, which used to be living things that got buried and cooked by the Earth. Story, story, story.

Even the electricity that makes the computer work has a story. Ours comes from a power station that uses coal. Coal comes from the ground, but it used to be plants—moss and giant ferns and trees that were alive before my Nanna was born, and she was born a million years ago. Well, I might be exaggerating there. Just a little. My Nanna is actually sixty-four, and there aren't any dinosaurs in the background of the photos of her as a child.

The "thing" that this story is about isn't in the background of the photos of my Nanna either—it's in the foreground. Nanna says that you can see it hanging around her neck in every shot since she was ten years old. Look closely.

Yes, that's it—the pendant. She still wears it. That tiny black eye has seen more of the world than any living thing. There's a story in it. A huge story. My Nanna has been telling me the story before I go to sleep. When you're twelve, you're supposed to be too old for bedtime stories, but there are some that go on and on and suck you right in. She's been telling me for a month, and she's nowhere near the end. It's a horror story and a love story at the same time, layered like fossils with history, suspense, and mystery. Get comfy. Hang on. You never know where we might end up.

It would make sense to start at the beginning, but how far back should we go? Nanna says the stone in the pendant came from a mine in the desert, but it was obviously in the Earth for a long time before that. Maybe I should stick to the history my Nanna knows. In her words.

"The mine where the stone was found started off as an underground house. In the early 1900s, when people rode their horses and carts out into the desert looking for new places to live, there were no trees to build houses from, but they desperately needed a place to get out of the sun. They dug in the hard rocky ground, sweating and toiling, until they made a shelter. Hand-made caves you could call them.

"One of the early settlers was named Billy Bobby Burton. An unfortunate name, but a name people tend to remember. Billy Bobby Burton was as strong as a horse and almost as big. He dug up the pale ground like a machine and carved himself a lovely room. It stayed cool during the day and was warm at night when the desert grew very cold.

"On one of Mr. Burton's trips to the big city, he met a beautiful girl. Her name was Christina, and Billy Bobby Burton fell in love with her in an instant. Her eyes sparkled like drops of dew in the morning sun, and when she said his name it sounded like a poem. Billy Bobby Burton asked her to marry him, and to his absolute delight, she said yes. They got married the next day, and then Christina packed her suitcase and went to live with Mr. Burton in the desert.

"Billy Bobby Burton's house wasn't big enough for the two of them, but one of the lovely things about living underground is that, if you want another room, you just dig one. Billy Bobby Burton dug a kitchen where his lovely wife could bake cakes and a bathroom where his lovely wife could wash in the water he collected from the well and a bedroom where his lovely wife could sleep."

Nanna paused and then shook her head slowly.

"What?" I asked. "What happened?"

"While Billy Bobby Burton was putting the final touches on the bedroom ceiling, he uncovered a stone so dark that it looked as though he'd dug straight through to the night sky between the stars. No larger than one of his big old coins, the rock fascinated the man, and he gently chipped it from the roof by candlelight."

Nanna stopped again and stared at me.

"What?"

"As the dark stone came free, so did a huge boulder."

I swallowed, and it made a funny squeak.

"Billy Bobby Burton never saw the dark stone by the light of day."

"He died?"

"No! No, for goodness' sake, no. The boulder hit his head and struck him blind. Billy Bobby

Burton never saw his beautiful wife again either. I mean, she was in love with the man, so she didn't stray far, but Mr. Burton's *eyes* never worked again, so he . . . you know what I mean."

"Yes, of course," I said. "What happened to the stone?"

"That, my dear, is another story."

"No! That's not fair!"

"Perhaps, but that's the way of the world. Sometimes it seems unfair. We'll continue the story tomorrow night."

"What if you die?"

Nanna laughed out loud. "I'm not going to die, Ben. I promise."

CHAPTER 2
THE STONE BECOMES AN EYE

I could hear Mom and Nanna talking in the kitchen while I brushed my teeth. Mom was saying how she'd miss Nanna when she was gone.

"It's so easy to get Ben to go to bed while you're around," Mom said. "How do you do it?"

There was a pause, and then Nanna said, "There are things I have to tell him before I go."

"Things? What things?"

"Family secrets."

"Oh, I see."

"It seems like he's as ready to hear them as I am to tell them."

I spat toothpaste into the sink and dove into bed. She was coming.

She closed my bedroom door behind her, but not completely. She rolled my desk chair over and sat close.

"Where was I?" she whispered.

"Billy Bobby Burton was blinded by the boulder," I said.

Her eyes widened. "You remembered his name!"

"Of course. It's a name people tend to remember, remember?"

"Indeed," she said and folded her hands together on her lap.

I snuggled into my pillow. I was ready all right.

Nanna sighed. "Poor Billy Bobby Burton. When Christina found him on the floor of their new bedroom, he had blood on his brow and the dark stone clutched in his fingers. She called for help, and their neighbor, a toothless man everyone called Jingo Jim, came running. He loaded Billy Bobby Burton and Christina into his cart and dashed off to the hospital in the city."

"Was Billy ok?"

Nanna nodded. "Blind, but otherwise ok. He didn't see who took the dark stone from his hand. Neither did Christina; she was so worried about her husband."

"Who took it?"

"What do you think?"

"Jingo Jim?"

Nanna grinned. "Yes! He took the stone and told himself it was a fair trade for bringing Billy Bobby Burton and his lovely wife to the city."

"He just *took* it?"

Nanna shrugged. "Some people feel like they need to be paid for every little thing they do. Some people aren't as generous as others."

"*I* wouldn't have taken it," I said.

Nanna patted my hand. "That's because you are an honest person, Ben. Not only did Jingo Jim take the stone, when he heard that Billy Bobby Burton had been blinded by the accident, he offered to buy Mr. Burton's underground house. He knew a blind man would be better in the city than in the desert."

"That . . . That's a *kind* thing to do, isn't it?"

"Jingo Jim offered them six shillings for their house."

"Oh. That doesn't sound like much."

"No, it wasn't. Not even in the old, old days. Christina had arranged for them to live in the apartment at the back of her father's house in the city—just until they found their feet. They took the six shillings offered. As it turned out, they only lived in the apartment for seven months. Blind Billy Bobby Burton used some of the six shillings to take piano lessons. He had a fabulous ear for music and became one of the greatest piano players of the century."

"Really?"

Nanna nodded. "Look him up on the Internet one day. He and Christina had four sons and five daughters, and they all learned how to play the piano."

"What happened to the stone?"

"Well, Jingo Jim couldn't believe his luck. He had the mysterious stone, and he had the underground house where it was found. He guessed the stone was some sort of jewel, so he took it to the jeweler in the city, but the jeweler said it wasn't really worth anything. He offered him one penny for the rough rock, saying that he'd turn it into cheap earrings. Disappointed, Jingo Jim took the money and spent it on candy before heading home to the desert.

"When he got back to the desert, he found that an earthquake had caused his new six-shilling house to collapse, and his own home had crumbled as well. That's the downside of living underground. He dug it all out again, though, and he turned Billy Bobby's house into a mine. He dug for twenty-five years, but he didn't find any jewels or any more dark stones."

"Why would you bother?" I asked.

"Excuse me?"

"Why would you bother digging if you never found anything?"

"I didn't say he didn't find *anything*, just no jewels or dark stones."

"What *did* he find?"

"Dinosaur bones. Thousands and thousands of dinosaur bones. He has several dinosaurs named after him."

"Really?"

"Really."

"But that doesn't explain how the stone . . ."

Nanna held up her finger. "The jeweler had lied. He'd tricked Jingo Jim into believing that the dark stone was worthless, but in fact it was precious and extremely valuable. He knew that if he shaped and polished the gem, it would be worth a lot of money. He was laughing to himself as he started working on it. Maybe it was the laughing that made him lose his concentration while he was using the stone cutter."

Nanna looked me right in the eye, her face blank.

"What happened?"

"The jeweler was sucked into the machine."

I gasped out loud. "He was *killed?*"

"Oh, goodness no. It just nipped the top of his little finger off. A bit of blood. His fingernail grew a bit crooked after that, but he was ok."

"What about the stone?"

"The dark rock was now a gemstone of great beauty. It was almond-shaped, like an eye or a teardrop. He fashioned it into the centerpiece of a golden brooch. It was truly beautiful. The pride and joy of the jeweler's collection."

Nanna sighed.

"And?"

"And what?"

"And what did he do with it?"

"That, my dear, is another story."

"Noooo! More. Tell me more."

"Perhaps tomorrow night."

"You're so cruel!"

Nanna grinned. "Sometimes people seem cruel even when they have your best interests at heart."

"What's that supposed to mean?"

Nanna touched her nose, smiled, and then kissed my cheek. "Tomorrow," she whispered.

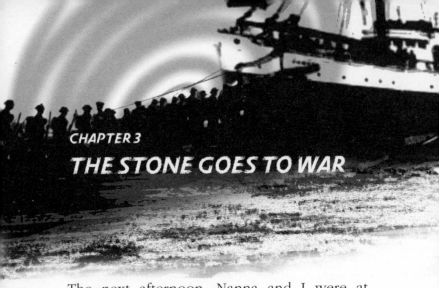

CHAPTER 3

THE STONE GOES TO WAR

The next afternoon, Nanna and I were at the library, and I remembered what she had said about Billy Bobby Burton being a famous piano player. I searched for him on the computer and found 11,000 pages that mentioned him. He was famous all right, especially in the early 1900s. He toured the world for thirty-nine years, had four sons and five daughters, and played the blues. They called him Blind Billy. There was no mention of the underground house in the desert or the dark stone, but I guessed there were bigger things in his life.

"How do you know all this stuff?" I asked Nanna.

"What do you mean?"

"About the stone. About Billy Bobby Burton. It all happened before you were born."

Nanna touched the pendant that hung around her neck. "My mother told me."

"*Your* mother?"

She nodded. "Your great-grandmother Elise. She knew everything about everything, or so it seemed."

"Did she write a book? She should have written a book. *You* should write a book," I suggested.

She took my arm. "You can never write these stories down, Ben. Do you hear me?"

"I . . . I . . . Ok. Why not?"

She fingered the pendant again. Her voice became a sharp whisper. "There are people out there who would love to get their hands on the stone—descendants of those who held the stone but lost it. People who wrongly believe that the stone belongs to them."

I nodded, pretending that I understood, and we left the library in silence.

Over dinner that night, the adults had one of those strange adult conversations that aren't supposed to concern me but that I can't help listening to.

My dad started it all with a simple question. "How's Dad doing?" he asked Nanna.

She'd been on the phone with Grandpa that evening. I was watching TV at the time, but I could hear her crying quietly as she spoke with him.

"He's ok. It won't be long now."

Grandpa worked for the army. He was away a lot. When my mom was young, they used to all travel together, but they got sick of all the different houses. That's why Nanna lived with us. We weren't allowed to know where Grandpa was going or when he'd be back. It was top secret. Nanna missed him. We all did. He'd been overseas for more than a year this time. Nanna had been saying that he *wouldn't be long now* for months.

"How's he doing with that thing . . . that thing he's doing?" Dad asked.

"He thinks he's made it worse."

"Really? That's no good."

Nanna shrugged. "He always said it would have to get worse before it got better."

That concerned me. I'd seen the news. When the army makes things worse, people sometimes get hurt. Innocent people. Kind people like my grandpa.

Nanna tickled me playfully so I'd hurry into bed that night. It was past my bedtime, and she kissed my cheek and went to turn out my light.

"Nanna?" I called. "Haven't you forgotten something?"

"Have I?"

I patted my desk chair, still beside the bed.

"Oh, Ben. It's too late tonight. Double story tomorrow night."

"Ahem," I coughed and patted the chair again.

Her shoulders dropped. She sat down, and I snuggled deeper under the covers.

"The jeweler loved that stone. He treasured it for many years. He couldn't bear to sell it. He only loved one thing more than the stone and that was the girl from the bakery next door. Her name was Angelina Angel, and she had the cutest button nose and the longest, shiniest brown hair the jeweler had ever seen. The highlight of the jeweler's day was watching her take her hair down as she left work in the afternoon. If he was with a customer, he'd excuse himself and race out the front door onto the street.

"'Good afternoon, Miss,' he'd say. She'd smile, but she never said a word. This went on for more than a year. Every afternoon, the jeweler would call out his greeting, and Angelina Angel would smile at him but never say a word, until that one afternoon when everything changed."

Nanna paused for too long.

"And?" I said.

"Patience, Ben. A story worth telling has to be told properly, with care and sensitivity."

I moaned.

Nanna smiled. "Just as Angelina left work on that fateful day, the heavens opened up and bombarded the people on the street with hailstones. I mean, they didn't die or anything, but some of the more fine-skinned ladies were bruised by the falling pellets of ice.

"The jeweler hurriedly ushered Angelina Angel inside his dark shop. Her hair was still tucked into her baker's cap, and she didn't let it down. She shook the hail off her cap and stared at the weather through the window.

"'Come,' the jeweler said. 'Come and sit with me awhile. The storm won't last long. Perhaps I can make you a cup of tea?'

"Angelina Angel shook her head and pointed outside. The jeweler stepped behind the counter and rummaged through a drawer. 'You must,' he said. 'I have something for you.' Angelina shook her head and waved her hand. 'It is very beautiful,' the jeweler insisted. 'Just as you are.'

"Angelina blushed and pushed at the door, but the jeweler had locked it. He laughed, but it wasn't a kindly laugh. Angelina pointed along the street and then held her hands as if she were praying to the jeweler. 'What is it, my dear?' he said. 'Does the cat have your tongue?'

He moved across the room, his hand clenched into a fist."

Nanna stopped and stared at me.

"*And?*" I demanded. "And?"

"Dramatic pause, Benjamin. Dramatic pause."

"Arghhh!"

"The jeweler thrust out his downturned fist and left it hanging in the air. He shook it. Angelina Angel tentatively put out her hand, and he dropped the gold brooch onto her palm and closed her fingers around it. 'Beauty for a beauty,' he whispered.

"The hail had stopped as quickly as it had started, so the jeweler unlocked the door, and Angelina Angel sprang into the street. She pushed the brooch into her pocket without looking at it. 'Aren't you even going to look at it?' the jeweler called, but Angelina Angel shrugged and ran toward the dock. 'Come back!' he screamed. 'Thief! Help! Police! She stole my brooch!'"

"But she *didn't* steal it," I protested.

"Exactly," Nanna said. "Far from it. The police didn't catch her. Melting hail crunched under her shoes as she ran for the wharf. She pushed her way through the crowd to where soldiers were boarding a giant steamboat. She looked at every face and started to cry."

"Who was she looking for? Why was she crying?"

Nanna held up her finger.

"Then she saw him. It was Samuel Stetson, with his golden hair tucked under his army hat and his smooth, tanned forearms peeking out from his shirtsleeves. He was almost at the gangplank, almost boarding the boat that would take him away, possibly forever. It was the beginning of World War I, and Samuel Stetson's battalion was sailing for Europe. Samuel Stetson was Angelina Angel's sweetheart, and she'd never told him that she loved him. She'd never told him anything."

"Anything? But he was her sweetheart."

Nanna shook her head. "She'd never told him a single thing because Angelina Angel couldn't speak. She was born that way, and she'd never said a word, but Samuel Stetson knew that she loved him."

"How? How did he know if she didn't tell him?"

"Ah, there are things that speak of love with a purer voice than words."

"Such as what?"

"Such as eyes. They saw each other, and it was as if the crowd parted just for them. They held on tight to each other and cried and cried.

"Soon it was time for Samuel Stetson to board the ship. He took a small velvet box from his pocket and pressed it into Angelina Angel's hand. It was a locket. A golden locket containing a tiny black and white picture of Samuel Stetson in uniform and a snip of his golden hair.

"Angelina Angel wished she'd thought to get something for Samuel Stetson, and then she remembered the gift the jeweler had given her. She dug it from her pocket, having not truly seen it, and gave it to Samuel Stetson. He looked puzzled and delighted with that dark stone eye nestled in gold. A beautiful and unusual gift from his beautiful and unusual sweetheart.

"He held it to his heart. 'I'll be back,' he promised her. She blew him a kiss. He was swept aboard the ship. Angelina Angel couldn't bear to watch him leave."

"They never saw each other again," I said.

"What? No!" Nanna said. "Hardly. Angelina Angel joined the war effort as a baker and was shipped off to France to cook for the soldiers. She and Samuel Stetson got married during the war. When the war ended, they settled in London and started a bakery and a family."

"What about the brooch?"

Nanna's mouth curled into a sly smile. "That, my dearest, is another story."

"Ohhh! I can't believe it. You are unreal!"

Nanna laughed as she turned out the light, and it wasn't a very kindly laugh.

CHAPTER 4

IN THE TRENCHES

We went to a movie on Thursday night. It's one of our family rituals. I don't remember the name of the movie we saw, which doesn't mean I didn't like it. It was great. It was a love story set during the war. I kept thinking about Samuel Stetson, Angelina Angel's sweetheart, ducking mortar fire and digging trenches to hide from the enemy's machine guns.

At one point in the movie, the hero, a young man named Michael, was in a wet and muddy trench in the flashing dark. Something hit him hard on the shoulder, and in the gloom, he saw that it was an enemy grenade. He tried to pick it up, but it was slippery. He heaved it away just in the nick of time. Nanna's nails dug into my arm during that scene.

"What do you mean, I owe you a story?" Nanna said as she tucked me into bed that night.

"For nearly making my arm bleed during the movie."

Nanna chuckled. "Sorry about that. It's late. More story tomorrow night."

"Just a short one," I pleaded.

"Sleep," Nanna said.

She turned out the light, and I pretended to cry.

"Oh, hush, you baby," Nanna growled, but she turned the light back on again and settled herself on the chair.

I pulled my blankets up to my chin like a little kid.

"It was 1915. Samuel Stetson's battalion was positioned in the trenches near Ypres in Belgium. The fighting there was some of the most horrible in the whole war. The Germans filled the battalion's trenches with poison gas, and Samuel Stetson had to have a gas mask on hand at all times. Every day, as the morning sun revealed the gruesome sights of the battlefield again, Samuel Stetson took the brooch Angelina Angel had given him from his pocket, kissed it for luck, and tucked it safely away again. He reminded himself of his promise to come back to her and carried out the brutal work of a soldier with every bit of his strength."

"He kept his promise," I said.

Nanna nodded once. "Without that promise and the brooch, Samuel Stetson would have given up and died. His trench was captured, and Samuel was taken as a prisoner of war. They were marched through the rain, deep into enemy territory, and locked in an old church.

"The German soldiers seized their guns and their papers. Samuel Stetson hoped they wouldn't find the brooch, but the German captain was a thorough man. He found the tiny lump in Samuel's pocket and took the precious stone. Samuel Stetson was heartbroken, but the promise he made to Angelina Angel kept him strong. Later, in his makeshift office at the rear of the church, the captain admired the jewel by candlelight. He wanted to keep it, but he knew he couldn't."

"He had to give it back to Samuel Stetson," I said.

"That would have been the right thing to do, but this was wartime, and more horrible things than stealing brooches went on during the war. No, the captain couldn't keep the dark stone because he had a sweetheart, too. He knew she wouldn't have seen anything as beautiful as that brooch because she was a poor Belgian farmer's daughter.

"Her name was Hannah Harper. She may have come from a poor family, but she was the most beautiful woman the captain had ever seen. She spoke mostly Flemish, and he spoke mostly German, but he knew that the gift of the brooch would say more than words ever could."

"Like Angelina Angel," I said.

Nanna patted my hand. "Exactly! The German captain and the Belgian farmer's daughter were on different sides during the war, though. If they were caught together, there would be serious trouble, so they met in secret, after dark, by the fountain in the square.

"Early in 1916, on the spring night of their last meeting, the captain stole away from his post and gave Hannah Harper the golden brooch. She fell instantly in love with the dark stone, but she didn't love the captain. He just wasn't her type. She tried to give the beautiful thing back to him, but the captain wouldn't take it. She tried to explain that the gift was too much, that she didn't deserve it, but the captain couldn't understand. He became frustrated and shouted at Hannah Harper, and that attracted the attention of the guards on duty. Hannah Harper took off her shoes and ran silently into the night."

"Did the guards catch her?" I asked.

"Very nearly. She ducked into a blind alley and the troops marched by. One guard even shone a light down the lane where she was hiding and still didn't see her."

I sighed out loud.

"Yes, it was a close call for Hannah Harper. She crept home in the early hours of the morning, and her father was waiting for her. He'd waited all night, and he demanded to know where she had been. He said he knew she was meeting the German soldier and that they could never meet again if she valued her life.

"The farmer had heard whispers that the Germans were losing the war. He feared for his daughter. He had no idea what would happen to her if the Germans lost, but he wasn't about to sit around and watch. He loved her too much for that.

"Hannah Harper explained to her father that she didn't love the German captain, that he wasn't her type but that he had insisted on giving her bread . . . the bread that had kept Hannah Harper and her family alive through the hard winter. The farmer nodded his understanding and told his daughter that he wished she could go find a life for herself in a place that hadn't been torn apart by war. It hurt him to say it, but he wished she were safe somewhere on the other side of the world."

"Why didn't she just get on a plane?" I asked.

"There weren't many planes in those days, and those few that existed were being used to fight the war. If you wanted to get anywhere overseas, you had to travel by boat."

"Why didn't she just get on a boat then?"

Nanna held up one finger to quiet me. "It was never that simple during the war. Besides, Hannah Harper didn't want to leave her family, but in the end she had to."

"Why?"

"Because, later that morning, the guards came to the farmhouse looking for her. The German captain knew where she lived, and even if it did cause trouble, he wanted her to be his wife.

"Hannah kissed her mother, her father, and her two brothers goodbye and snuck out the back door. She hopped from bomb crater to bomb crater until she was in the burnt and deserted remains of the forest behind the farm. She stumbled from broken town to broken town, avoiding patrols and heading for the border with France—heading for the Western Front where the war truly showed its teeth. Then, with the Western Front in sight, Hannah Harper felt a tearing pain in her leg and fell to the muddy ground."

"What? She died?" I asked.

"Eventually, yes."

"Oh. That's not a very nice story."

"She didn't die at the Western Front, no. She died many years later, as we all do. On that day, she was shot in the thigh. She had lost a lot of blood when the Allied soldiers found her, and she was treated in a field hospital by a medic from New Zealand. He spoke to her soothingly, but she couldn't understand a word he was saying. Hannah Harper only knew a few words in English—just 'please' and 'thank you' and how to count to ten.

"The medic couldn't speak Flemish at all, and his school French only confused her. That all changed when a Belgian soldier arrived at the field hospital. He had suffered a broken arm, but he spoke both Flemish *and* English. He interpreted for the medic and the farm girl, and the three of them chatted long into the night. Hannah Harper explained that she needed to leave Belgium because the German captain wanted to marry her, and the medic concocted a plan to get her out of war-torn Europe altogether.

"They cut off Hannah's beautiful hair and dressed her in a spare uniform. They bandaged her face so that nobody would know she was a woman. Then the medic wrote a sign to hang around Hannah Harper's neck that said, 'This brave soldier has breathed gas in the trenches and cannot speak.'

"The medic gave her his identification papers and sent her off on the first ship to New Zealand. It took months to cross the great oceans. Hannah Harper held the brooch given to her by the German captain and wondered if she had done the right thing.

"Her leg got better, and by the time the ship docked in Wellington harbor, Hannah had swapped her army uniform for a dress. She pretended to be a nurse and hid her short hair under a nurse's cap. She made beds, fed wounded soldiers, and never said a word she didn't have to. She helped move the wounded ashore and disappeared into the crowd when her work was done."

"Just disappeared?" I asked.

"Not literally, dear, no. She wandered around the city in a daze for the best part of a day. She had no money and nowhere to sleep. She'd learned a few more words of English on the ship but not enough to change her fortunes. She had only one possession of any value and that was the brooch the German captain had given her. She realized that she'd have to sell it to survive in this strange place. On Willis Street, not far from the harbor, she stumbled upon a building leased by the Dwan brothers, pawnbrokers."

"What's a pawnbroker?"

"Somebody who loans you money and keeps your goods until you repay the loan with interest. You want a two dollar loan, and they hold on to your watch, that sort of thing."

I rubbed my hands together. "Perfect!"

"Well, in a manner of speaking, yes, but pawnbrokers are notoriously shrewd. They make a living out of wheeling and dealing, so they have to be good at striking a bargain in their own favor."

"Uh-oh."

"Mmm. The pawnbroker in question had never met the daughter of a Belgian farmer before, and Hannah Harper was no fool when it came to money. One of the Dwan brothers made the mistake of looking closely at the brooch, and like all who truly see it, he fell in love with the thing. Using broken English and numbers written on a scrap of paper, Hannah Harper pawned the beautiful brooch for 316 dollars."

"Whoah! That sounds like a lot."

"It was. She would never be able to pay it back, but it was enough for Hannah to buy a small dairy farm just outside of Wellington and to pay for her family to come and join her after the war. Unfortunately, her father became sick and died on the journey to New Zealand, but her mother and two brothers survived the trip, and their ancestors still work at the same farm."

"That's it?"

"What?"

"That's the end of the story?"

"Hannah Harper's part in it, yes."

"Don't tell me . . . The rest is another story."

Nanna just grinned and kissed my forehead. "How did you guess?"

CHAPTER 5

YOU WIN SOME, YOU LOSE SOME

Nanna spoke to Grandpa again on Friday after school. I couldn't hear what she was saying, even listening with my super-spy ears (which are the same as my regular ears, just straining to eavesdrop).

I couldn't hear what they were talking about, but she wasn't crying. Far from it. Nanna was laughing. Laughing like Amber-Grace Tomlinson from school—the kind of laugh that infects you like a disease and you smile and then start laughing yourself. Mr. Jensen calls Amber-Grace a "giggle goose," but he can't stop himself from laughing when she gets going. Yes, well, Nanna's a giggle goose, too.

To make matters worse—like scratching a mosquito bite—when Nanna got off the phone, she went straight to Mom and started whispering. Arghhh! I hate that. How am I supposed to overhear military secrets if the spies are always mumbling under their breath? That's not very fair.

Nanna tucked me in that night.

"So how's Grandpa?" I asked casually.

"He's . . . He's fine. He's well. Sends his love."

"How are the unmentionable things going in Unmentionable Land?"

Nanna chuckled. "Unmentionably well . . . or badly. I can't really say."

I moaned.

"You know the rules, Ben. I'd tell you if it weren't a matter of national security."

"When Grandpa goes to the bathroom it's a matter of national security!"

Nanna snorted. "Matter of national emergency, more like." She grabbed the pendant hanging around her neck and stared off into the distance. "We all miss him."

We were silent for a while, thinking our lonesome thoughts about Grandpa.

"Did Grandpa give you the stone?" I asked.

"No, my mother did."

"Great-grandmother Elise?"

"Yes. You remembered!"

"Why is it a necklace? When you tell the story, it's always a brooch."

"It *was* a brooch, but let's not get ahead of ourselves."

Nanna sat, and I snuggled under the covers. She took a breath.

"The twin Dwan brothers, the pawnbrokers, were opposites in every way. Kip, the older brother by two minutes, was mousy-haired and lumpy with muscles. He never brushed his teeth or his hair, and it showed, but he was notoriously good at lifting heavy things. Jed, his twin, cut a fine figure in a suit, wore his dark hair parted down the middle, and was really the brains of the operation. Oh, and his teeth shone. Quite literally. A fall from a swing as a boy had chipped Jed's front tooth, and as soon as he was rich enough to do so, he had the chip covered with a crown of pure gold.

"Their business did a brisk trade, and Jed's eye for math had made them both very wealthy.

However, their affluence came at a price . . . Nobody really liked them. Jed and Kip weren't good at being friends with others, and they sat on their own in the cafés until someone new came to town. That's where they met Frank Feer, a fast-talking Texan who liked to play cards.

"Well, if they'd had national poker championships in those days, more than likely Jed would have been the best in New Zealand, but New Zealand isn't America, and Frank Feer had a few tricks up his sleeve. Every Friday for a month, Jed and Frank met in Wentworth's Hotel and played five-card stud. It's a simple game, but the stakes were high, and Frank Feer lost fistfuls of money. More than a hundred dollars in all."

"I thought you said Frank Feer had tricks up his sleeve."

"Oh, he did. He was secretly very good. So good, in fact, that he deliberately lost money for a whole month, knowing that when the time was right, he stood a good chance of winning it all back *and* a whole lot more besides.

"So Frank Feer played and lost until Jed Dwan began thinking that Friday night poker meant easy money. Frank won a couple of hands, then a couple more, and he started to win some of his money back. He knew that Jed was ripe for the picking when he sensed the pawnbroker getting angry over his losses.

"Jed slammed his glass on the table. 'Perhaps we should call it a night?' Frank Feer suggested. 'No!' growled Jed Dwan. 'We're not finished yet.' They played some more, and Jed won a big hand, which had exactly the effect Frank Feer knew it would."

"What was that?"

"Jed got greedy. He saw his pile of money growing fatter again and felt that it was only a matter of time before he cleaned the Texan out, so they played on late into the night. The stakes just kept getting bigger. They attracted quite a crowd. Soon the music had stopped, and all the people in the hotel crowded around Jed and Frank's table and held their breath as the bets were made.

"Finally, Frank Feer bet every last cent on one hand. In order to match the bet, Jed Dwan had to empty his brother's pockets and dig deep into his own. He had put the brooch there in his pocket in case of emergency, and now he fingered it and looked at his cards. He had a full house—three kings and two queens. A good hand. No, a *great* hand. So he showed Frank Feer the brooch and offered it as his final bet. Frank knew jewelry and could see, in one glance, that the stone was worth a small fortune. He accepted the bet. Whoever won this hand, won everything."

Nanna raised her eyebrows at me. Then she stood and kissed my brow. "Goodnight, darling. We'll finish this story tomorrow."

"No!" I bellowed. I jumped out from under my sheets and grabbed her in a hug, dragging her back to her seat.

She was laughing. "I was only teasing! No need to get rough."

"You are so *mean*!"

We settled again, and Nanna leaned in close. "Jed revealed his full house, one card at a time, and sat back in his chair, quietly confident. The crowd craned forward to look, gasped, and then cheered. Frank Feer stared at the cards on the table, and Jed began to chuckle, his gold tooth glinting in the lantern light.

"Then Frank spread his fan of cards neatly at the base of the money pile. The crowd cheered all over again. Four aces. Frank had won. All of the blood drained from Jed Dwan's face, and he hurried from the hotel. Kip watched as all of the money his brother had lost, and the beautiful stone, was raked into a pile and stuffed into a bag. He hoped his brother never played cards again.

"Frank Feer moved fast. He tucked the bag under his arm, and as he did so, several cards slipped from his sleeve."

It was my turn to gasp. "He'd *cheated?*"

Nanna nodded. "He'd collected the aces over several hands, secreting them up his sleeve, and on the final hand, he'd swapped his useless cards for the stash of big ones. The swapped cards fell to the table in full view of everybody, including Kip Dwan. In an instant, Kip knew his brother had been duped, and he dove at Frank Feer, but Frank was already running for the door. The chase went on long into the night.

The townspeople didn't like the pawnbrokers, but they liked cheaters even less, and Frank Feer found himself running for his life."

"Did they get him?"

"That, my dear, is another . . ."

"No! Just tell me . . . Yes or no?"

"If I tell you now, I won't know where to start next time I tell you a story."

"Yes you will! I'll remind you."

"Ah, but this way you'll be hungry for the next part."

"I'm already hungry!"

Nanna kissed my forehead, smiling. "Goodnight, Ben."

I pulled the blankets over my head.

"Goodnight, Ben," she said again.

So what if it was late. So what if I was tired. This was just cruel, but she was right about one thing—I'd be hungry for the next installment.

"Goodnight, Nanna."

CHAPTER 6
MONKEY BUSINESS

My friend Jack came over early on Saturday morning. I'd had breakfast, but I was still in my pajamas.

"Get changed," he said, instead of hello. "We're going to Nathan's. We're building the treehouse."

He had his sister's bike—the pink one with the basket on the front—and the basket was loaded with stuff: wood, two hammers, and a length of old rope.

I got changed in a hurry. We'd been talking about the treehouse for months, planning and collecting wood and nails and plastic. Well, Nathan and Jack had been collecting. I'd been planning. I'm much better at thinking things through than doing them. They are the doers.

Mom and Dad were watching TV in bed when I was ready to leave. I told them about our plans and that I'd be back after lunch.

"Do you need any tools?" Dad asked.

"Nathan already has the tools," I said.

"Be careful," Mom said.

It turns out that I'm not such a bad doer after all. Nathan called me the bald monkey. (I have plenty of hair on my head, but not as much as a monkey on my arms.) Anyway, I think he was referring to my climbing ability. I began making excuses to climb up and down the tree. I had discovered that I was next-to-useless with the saw and downright dangerous with the hammer, but I could get to the top of the tree in record time.

After that, Jack and Nathan cut and hammered, and I collected the wood from the ground and dragged it up to the work site. They had built a platform up there, only there wasn't enough room on it for three people. It felt rickety with *one* boy on board, but they both managed to find a place. They erected a sort of tent pole arrangement in the middle and hung the plastic over the top. It was neat but only built for two.

"You can be the lookout," Jack told me.

"*First* lookout," Nathan added. "You take the first lookout shift sitting in the branches up there, and then in a while we can switch with you, and you can go up to the hut, and Jack can be the lookout."

I was quite happy as the lookout. I could see across the road and way down to the park at the end of Prince Street. It looked like a jungle down there, a good place for a monkey to hide.

When I got home, there was a note taped to my bedroom door—Nanna apologizing for having to leave early. She said she'd be back tomorrow.

"Where has Nanna gone?" I asked Mom.

"I'm not sure exactly. She said she was meeting a friend and that they were going to be late, so not to wait up for her."

"It's like having a teenager in the house," Dad said.

I agreed, but at least she'd left a note.

We watched a DVD that night—Mom and Dad and I. Nanna's recliner was empty, so I jumped on that and kicked the footrest out.

"Be careful she doesn't catch you sitting there," Dad said.

"I don't care," I said. "She owes me anyway."

"Owes you?"

"Yes. She didn't tell me a story."

Dad chuckled. "Poor little baby didn't get his bedtime story," he teased.

I pretended to cry, and Dad laughed harder.

"What is she telling you about?" Mom asked.

It wasn't until Mom wanted to know that I realized I didn't want to say. It was something that just Nanna and I shared. I didn't want to try and explain, didn't want to start a story that I couldn't finish. "Oh, nothing much. A little bit of adventure. A little bit of mystery. This and that."

Mom rubbed the back of my hand. "Your grandmother is a great storyteller. She sucks you in, doesn't she?"

I nodded. Sucked me into a secret world, a family saga. If Nanna were home right now, I thought, I'd rather be tucked in bed listening to the next part of the story than watching this dull movie. That was just plain weird. I normally *love* a good movie, but somehow Nanna's tale had grown roots in my head, snaky roots that curled into my brain and held on tight. The DVD wasn't as *real* as Nanna's story.

It was eleven o'clock by the time I went to bed. I was tired, but the empty chair beside my bed got me thinking. Did Jed and Kip Dwan catch up with Frank Feer? If they caught him, Kip would probably tear him apart. Cheating them out of their money and the brooch was a totally brave and totally stupid thing for Frank Feer to do.

I imagined Frank running off into the wilderness and eventually reappearing in a new town with a new identity. He probably bought a mansion with eighty-seven rooms, had big parties that went on for days, and had friends over for sleepovers every night of the week. Well, that's what I would have done, anyway.

CHAPTER 7
MORE MONKEY BUSINESS

I got the surprise of my life on Sunday morning. I slept in, and when I woke up around eleven o'clock, the house was full of activity. Grandpa was home.

I couldn't help myself when I saw him; I ran at him like I was three years old. He swept me off my feet and spun me around the living room until I kicked one of the couch cushions onto the floor and Mom growled at us. He kissed my cheek with his prickly face. He was so brown and healthy-looking. He looked younger than I remembered, but it was Grandpa all right.

We hugged, and he spun me some more, but then I couldn't think of what to say. I couldn't ask him how his work was, or anything like that, because he couldn't talk about it. I couldn't ask about the country where he was staying or about his adventures. I just stood there, giggling like a giggle goose.

Grandpa was shaking his head. His eyes were shiny, but he was smiling. "I can't believe how much you've grown, Benny boy." He held his thumb and first finger about an inch apart. "When I left, you were this big!"

I shrugged. "I can't help it. You've been away awhile."

He hugged me again. "You're right. Too long. Never mind, I'm home now."

"For how long?" I asked.

"Never mind about that," he said. "What have you been up to? What have I missed out on? Your mother tells me you've been making a treehouse with your friends."

We all sat around the living room and had a catch-up session, and the adults had about one hundred cups of tea. I looked over at Nanna at one stage, and she was grinning.

"What?" she said, when she saw me watching her.

"You're a cheeky monkey."

She made an "o" shape with her mouth and then winked. "That's me . . . cheeky monkey. Always up to some sort of monkey business."

Grandpa went to bed early—jetlag he said— so I had Nanna to myself at bedtime again. I thundered into my room after brushing my teeth and dove onto my bed.

When we were settled, she held the pendant and stared at the ceiling.

"Frank Feer ran from the Dwan brothers for a total of six minutes. He'd planned that part of his swindle to perfection. He dodged through the streets and lost Kip Dwan in the shadows. He backtracked past the fuming pawnbroker and down to the harbor. He slipped aboard the clipper ship he'd seen being loaded that afternoon and hid in a long wooden box that kept the sails out of the weather when they weren't in use. It was warm and relatively comfortable and safe from the wrath of the Dwan brothers.

"Frank Feer fell asleep and woke up again some time before dawn. As he'd anticipated, the clipper was on the open sea. They'd sailed at first light. Through the gap in the lid of his box, Frank could see the deckhands rushing around, tightening ropes, and shouting to each other in a language he didn't recognize.

"Half a day and goodness knows how many nautical miles passed before a crewman popped the lid off his box and found Frank Feer. Frank smiled and said hello. The man grabbed him roughly by his collar and dragged him up to the captain. Frank offered the captain money. (He'd stashed all but a few dollars in a safe place.) The captain smiled a broken-toothed grin. 'A stowaway becomes a deckhand and pays for the privilege,' he said. 'I like this story. Ha-ha-ha!'"

"Where were they sailing to?" I asked.

"Frank didn't know. He was beginning to wish he'd chosen another boat to stow away on. The captain and the crew worked him hard. They had him scrubbing the decks and climbing the rigging to adjust the sails. Luckily, Frank was a bit of a monkey, and he climbed with ease right up to the very top."

"Me, too," I said. "I could do that."

"You're not afraid of heights?"

"Nope," I said. "I love climbing."

"That doesn't surprise me at all, Ben. Your mother was a good climber, too."

"Really?"

Nanna nodded. "We couldn't keep her on the ground. She'd climb your grandfather if he stood still long enough!"

I'd never seen my mother climb anything but stairs, and she usually did that standing up.

"How are you at scrubbing decks?" Nanna asked.

"Ah, not so good, I guess."

"It doesn't sound like much fun, does it? It wasn't fun for Frank Feer either. He scrubbed until his hands and knees were red and raw. Every day seemed warmer than the last, and Frank realized that they were heading for somewhere in the tropics.

"Almost a month had passed since they left New Zealand, and the crew members were buzzing. Then Frank saw what all the fuss was about . . . They were approaching land. It was a massive island with a mist-covered mountain in the middle. Frank had traveled far and wide, but he'd never seen a place like it. As they drew closer, Frank speculated that it was one of the islands of Indonesia. He helped unload the clipper, collected his stash of cash and the brooch, and disappeared into the crowd.

"It was two days before Frank found anyone who spoke English on the tropical island. He met a trader from Holland who offered to exchange his poker winnings for local currency, so he did. Then he met a priest heading for the mountains. He was being pulled along in a cart by two local men, and he invited Frank to join his expedition. Frank Feer agreed and climbed aboard with the priest.

"Frank had been right when he thought the boat had landed in Indonesia. The priest told him they were heading for a village called Ubud and that they were on an island called Bali."

"Oh, I've heard of that!" I said. It took me a minute to remember where I'd heard of it, but it did come to me. "My friend Jack went there with his family over the holidays."

"Did he really? It's a very popular place for travelers these days, but back then not many visitors from outside the islands made it into the mountains. There were temples and rice fields and coconuts, and the local children flocked to see the strange men. The priest could speak the local language, and he helped Frank Feer buy fruit and chicken at the market in the middle of town.

"When Frank went to pay, the priest saw his stash of money and fainted. He fell down, right in the middle of the busy market. The priest had never seen so much money in his entire life. Oh yes, Frank was rich by anyone's standards. In the mountain village he became a sort of king, a kind and generous king. With the help of the priest and the local people, he built schools and houses for the poor. He gave the village its very first hospital, and he met a local girl. Her name was Yan, and she moved like the breeze through the market.

"After six months of mumbling greetings to each other, Frank had learned enough of the language to have a conversation with Yan. She was smart, and her father was a merchant in the village. They fell in love and were married in a temple near the monkey forest."

"*Monkey* forest?"

"Oh yes, there are many monkeys in the highlands of Bali. Hundreds of years ago, the locals built a temple for them in the jungle. They were considered both good luck and bad luck, and the shrine in the monkey forest was a popular place to be married.

"The ceremony was conducted by the priest who had brought Frank Feer to the village, and Frank gave his beloved Yan a special gift. That's right—a beautiful golden brooch, inlaid with a dark polished stone. He pinned it to her magnificent bridal dress, and when they were sitting down for a wedding photograph, a cheeky little monkey darted onto Yan's lap and stole the shiny brooch. The monkey tore it clean from her dress, leaving only the pin behind.

The wedding guests chased the monkey, but the little thing was too fast. It bolted to the top of a tree and disappeared."

"I would have climbed after it," I said.

"Some of the local boys *did* climb after it, but there were so many monkeys. The brooch was lost."

"How can *you* have it if it was lost to the monkeys?"

Nanna pressed the tip of my nose with a finger. "I think you already know the answer to that question."

I groaned and put on my best Nanna voice. "That, my dear, is another story."

My Nanna, the cheeky monkey, just smiled.

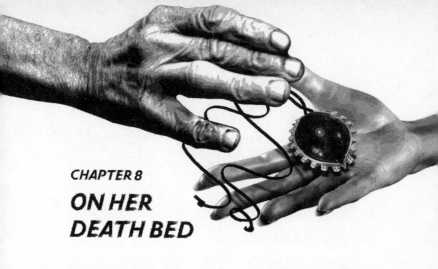

CHAPTER 8
ON HER DEATH BED

Grandpa cooked breakfast for everybody on Monday morning. I normally had a bowl of rice puffs before school, but Grandpa cooked up a storm with baked beans, fried tomatoes, bacon, mushrooms, and scrambled eggs, made with his own secret recipe. Top-secret recipe. Matter of national security.

I didn't have any mushrooms, but I ate everything else, including my plate. Well, almost everything else.

Jack and Nathan were whispering when I found them. As I got closer, they stopped talking altogether.

"What?" I asked.

"Nothing," Nathan said.

"We should tell him," Jack said, and he nudged Nathan.

"Tell me what?"

"We're planning a sleepover at Nathan's place," Jack said.

"Great! When?"

"Well, it was going to be this weekend, but . . ."

"But what?"

"You're not invited," Nathan said flatly.

I stared at the ground. "Thanks," I said and walked off. Jack chased me and grabbed my arm.

"It's not because we don't want you there," he said. "We're going to sleep in the treehouse, and you know . . . There's not really enough room for three."

"In the *treehouse*?" I said. "Are you crazy?"

"What? It's strong enough. Strong enough for two anyway," Nathan said.

I was disappointed, yes, but the thought of sleeping on that rickety frame at the top of the tree didn't thrill me. If I rolled over in the middle of the night, it would be like one of those flying dreams I have, only flying through the branches and landing on the ground would be a bit rougher than landing in my bed.

"That's ok," I said. "I understand."

It was the thought of the story that made it all ok. How strange was that? I normally *love* a sleepover. I'm always up for that sort of adventure, but if I had to choose between the wobbly, rickety treehouse, with Nathan snoring, and my own bed and Nanna's story, there was no contest. Nanna and the story would win every time.

"Really?" Jack asked.

"It's fine," I said. "Maybe it will be my turn next time."

"We're cool?" Nathan asked.

"Yes," I said. "Why wouldn't we be cool?"

"How about I tell you a story tonight, Ben?" Grandpa suggested.

"No offense, Grandpa, but Nanna's already halfway through a story," I said.

"Oh, I see," he said, crestfallen.

"You can stay and listen if you want."

Grandpa chuckled. "Thank you, but no. I'd better help your mother with the dishes."

In a way, I was glad he didn't want to stay. I love him, but the story was between Nanna and me.

I dove under my covers and waited. When Nanna arrived, she took my hand.

"This can't go on forever," she said.

"I know," I said. "It will have to end sooner or later. Every story has a beginning and a middle and an end."

"Very true."

"I think I know how this story ends anyway," I said and pointed to the pendant around her neck. It would have to get there somehow. Eventually.

"Ah, true, but there are endings that are nothing more than beginnings in disguise."

"What's that supposed to mean?"

Nanna touched the side of her nose. "You'll soon see."

She stared at my wall, gathering her thoughts. I held my breath.

"The monkeys of the monkey forest knew every rooftop and window in the village. They leapt from tree to tree to building in the early morning and snuck into houses and stole fruit from kitchens when people weren't looking. People got annoyed at the monkeys, but they didn't harm them. They just shooed them off with bamboo brooms if they caught them inside.

"There were some houses, however, where the monkeys were always welcome, where the owners collected food and welcomed them. One such house belonged to Ni Nyoman Nalami, an older woman with no family who shared her food with the monkeys. Sometimes, twenty-five monkeys would find their way inside her house. As you can imagine, the place was a mess. The monkeys would feed in the morning and trash the place. Then Ni Nyoman Nalami would clean up in the afternoon. The next day, the monkeys would be back again.

"Sometimes, Ni Nyoman Nalami's friends would ask her why she didn't just close the shutters on her house to stop the monkeys from coming inside, to which she replied, 'I will refuse the monkeys in my house only when they refuse me in theirs.'"

"Meaning?" I asked. I had an idea, but I had to be sure.

"Well, she meant that she'd lock the monkeys out of her house when they locked her out of the forest. Ni Nyoman Nalami loved the forest, and she loved the monkeys.

"Anyway, one day, one of the smallest monkeys in the troupe scampered onto the arm of her chair, as bold as can be, and took something gold from its mouth."

"The jewel."

Nanna nodded once. "Exactly. The little monkey dropped it into Ni Nyoman Nalami's hand and sprang, screeching, from the window back into the forest. Ni Nyoman Nalami cleaned the brooch carefully, but it was no longer a brooch. The pin was broken, and it could no longer be worn, so she threaded a length of fine leather through the remains of the latch and hung it around her neck."

"A pendant."

"Yes. She wore that stone every day for three years, feeling that it had been a special gift from the monkeys for her kindness toward them. Ni Nyoman Nalami was an old woman, though. She fell ill and was taken to the hospital, where the doctors gave her medicine and the nurses made her as comfortable as possible.

"Ni Nyoman Nalami knew she was dying. She befriended a kind-hearted nurse and told her the story of the monkey giving her the jewel. She gave the pendant to the nurse. It was Ni Nyoman Nalami's only real possession, and the nurse accepted it gracefully. That night, in the still of the early hours, Ni Nyoman Nalami breathed out for the last time. She was gone."

I felt my neck grow tight, and tears tickled at my eyes. I was sad for Ni Nyoman Nalami, but I was thinking about Nanna. What if the story didn't have an end? What if Nanna died before she could finish it? I sniffed.

"I know," Nanna said and held my hand. "It's sad, but everyone has to die. Eventually."

"I don't want to think about that," I said.

"Shhh. It's ok," she said. She patted my arm. "Pull yourself together. Worse things happen at sea, you know."

I wiped my face. "What do you mean?"

"It's a saying . . . 'Worse things happen at sea.' It means we must keep things in perspective. Sometimes losing something can be a blessing in disguise."

"Not if you're dead."

"Well, no, but the pendant wasn't dead. Far from it. The nurse wore it every day, and one day someone noticed it. An old priest. He saw the jewel and recognized it immediately as the one given by Frank Feer to his wife on their wedding day.

"'Where did you get that pendant?' the priest asked. 'One of our patients gave it to me,' she replied. 'Well, it wasn't hers to give,' said the priest. 'Give it to me.'

"The nurse held on to the pendant, and the priest grew angry. 'Give it to me,' he demanded. 'Or there will be trouble.'

"The nurse didn't fear the priest. He had gray hair growing out of his ears that made him look like he was wearing a crazy dance mask. She giggled and went back to her work.

"The priest told Frank Feer, and Frank went to the hospital and found the nurse wearing the pendant. He asked her about the jewel, and the nurse told him about Ni Nyoman Nalami and her kindness to the monkeys. Frank Feer, always the charmer, knew how to get what he wanted. He told the story of how the monkey stole the brooch, how it wasn't worth anything really, but it would mean a lot to his wife if he could return it to her.

"The nurse was touched by the story, and she reluctantly gave the pendant to Frank Feer. Frank had changed his ways since arriving in the mountains. He was a generous man now, and he gave the nurse some reward money. A *lot* of money. It wasn't as much as the jewel was worth, but it was enough for the nurse to buy a small home on the edge of a coconut grove.

"Frank Feer had the broken brooch remodeled by one of the jewelers in the village, and the brooch was now *officially* a pendant. He bought a startling gold chain and gave it to his wife for a second time.

"Yan loved the pendant, but she realized she loved the pendant more than she loved her husband. When Yan told her father of her unhappiness, the merchant advised her to leave the island to see the world. Yan's father was well traveled, and he knew his daughter shared his courage and fascination with new experiences.

"Frank Feer's wife left him on a lonely Thursday. She gave him back his wedding ring and told him that she was sorry but she had to leave. Something wasn't right in their house. Something wasn't right, and she blamed herself. She needed to see the world, as Frank himself had. She gave him the ring, but she kept the pendant.

"Her father gave her a small purse full of gold coins and arranged for her to leave the island secretly, as a passenger aboard a merchant vessel. In the smallest, darkest hours, when the tide was right, the boat left the harbor."

"Where was she going?" I asked.

"Yan didn't know," said Nanna with a smile.

I moaned. That, my dear, was another story.

"What about Frank Feer? What happened to him?"

"Frank's life unraveled at the seams. His sadness overwhelmed him, and he started playing cards again. He lost more money than he could make, and he was eventually chased from the village, carrying everything he owned tied in an old shirt."

"Really?"

Nanna nodded. "Perhaps not the most pleasant ending, but a true one just the same. Sometimes what goes around comes around. There are some who say Frank Feer got his comeuppance."

"Got what?"

"His just deserts. What he deserved."

"He only cheated the cheats, though. He was kind, and he built the hospital and all of that."

"True, but when you cheat a cheat, you become a cheat yourself."

I thought about that for a while. All of the good things Frank Feer brought to the mountain village—the school and the hospital and the housing—perhaps they were things he did to try and make himself feel better about swindling the money from the pawnbrokers in New Zealand. Perhaps he'd been lying to himself, trying to make up for his mistakes.

"Everybody deserves a second chance," I said.

"Indeed. For Frank Feer, it was more likely his tenth chance at making himself better, and he'd failed again. He saw the pattern of his life repeating, only this time, instead of running away from his problems, he walked into the mountains and studied Balinese Hinduism, a religion that teaches about *karma* and the idea that you will reap what you sow."

"Don't be mean to other people, or they'll be mean to you?"

"Yes, that's it. Also, if you show a little kindness, kindness comes back to you. They also believe in reincarnation—that, when you die, you might be reborn as another being."

"Did it work for Frank?"

"Oh yes. Frank Feer learned his lesson well. I think he came back as a monkey in the forest!"

Nanna kissed my forehead noisily and flicked the light out as she left.

I snuggled under my blankets. It would be cool to come back as a monkey.

CHAPTER 9

A RISING SUN

Grandpa cooked breakfast again on Tuesday. The rising sun made my window bright, but I slept in and only had time for one piece of toast before I had to leave for school. Everything smelled so good. I didn't want to go.

At school, Nathan and Jack were still talking sleepovers.

"I have one of those mega blocks of chocolate," Nathan said.

"Yesss," Jack hissed.

"Better not eat too much if there's a breeze," I suggested.

"Why not?" Jack asked.

I shrugged. "If you're up there, you might get seasick with a stomach full of chocolate and the treehouse swinging in the wind."

They laughed.

"I don't get seasick," Nathan said. "I get carsick, airsick, and boatsick, but I've never been seasick."

Jack grunted. "What's boatsick?"

"Yeah," I said. "How can you get boatsick but not seasick?"

"The boat down on the playground. The one on springs."

Jack screamed with laughter and slapped his thigh.

"Are you serious?" I asked.

Nathan nodded. "My sister was rocking it too hard. She wouldn't let me get off. I was sick all over her."

The bell rang, and we scuttled off to class, but Jack and I made sick noises all day. Nathan was Jacksick and Bensick by the end of it. His face turned a reddish-purple color, and he stopped talking to us. He has no sense of humor.

Our house was a web of whispers again after dinner that night. I pretended to watch television and listened as hard as I could, but nothing made much sense.

"It has to be your decision," Grandpa said aloud.

"Thank you very much," Nanna said, but she didn't sound very thankful.

When she came to tuck me into bed that night, I asked her, "What's your decision?"

"What do you mean?"

"Grandpa said it was your decision."

Nanna ignored the question. "Now, where were we? Ah yes, Yan Feer was aboard the ship, heading for who knows where . . ."

I hate it when adults do that. When they ignore my questions. Mr. Jensen pretends he's deaf if he doesn't want to talk about the things I want to know, but he doesn't do it just to me. Nathan raised his hand and asked him if God was real last month, and Mr. Jensen answered by talking about volcanoes and the layer of ash that covered Pompeii.

Anyway, even though being ignored and those kinds of answers annoy me, they can sometimes tell you more than if the person had answered normally. I could tell that Mr. Jensen didn't feel comfortable talking about God, and that Nanna didn't want to talk about the decision she had to make. I knew better than to push her.

"The ship sailed for the best part of a month. Poor Yan was seasick for the whole trip. It was rough out there. Monsoons chased them through Malaysia and the Philippines, across the South China Sea, and into the Sea of Japan. Eventually, they made it to the port of Fukuoka on the Japanese island of Kyushu. The vessel had only stopped to fill up with supplies before heading on to Tokyo, but Yan could travel no more. She was sick of being sick. She was a long way from home, and she didn't understand a word said to her, but with her feet on the ground and a sparkling new world to explore, she found ways to communicate.

"She swapped some of her father's gold coins for a pile of Japanese money. At the market, she pointed to the food she wanted to buy and played a sort of charades game whenever she needed help with other things. It was frustrating at times, but she was persistent and almost always got what she needed. The Japanese people were very patient with her.

"That all changed at the fish market one day when, over the hubbub of the crowd, Yan heard someone singing, 'I'm a little teapot, short and stout, here is my handle, here is my spout.' You see, Frank had been teaching his wife to speak English the whole time they'd been together, and that song had been one she'd learned. The singer in the market was a young woman named Tomomi Taiko, and they became the best of friends, talking to each other in broken English.

"Tomomi Taiko became Yan's guide, and together they traveled into the mountains of Kyushu on bicycles. They bathed in *onsen,* or hot springs, and slowly Yan began to learn the customs and the language. In the six months they traveled together, Tomomi and Yan grew inseparable.

"Tomomi was a beautiful and elegant dancer—the best in her school, she said. Once she'd seen her dance, Yan wanted Tomomi to dance all the time, but mostly they rode. They rode their bikes from one side of the island to the other. All the way to Kagoshima.

"On the dock in Kagoshima, Yan saw the ships and felt the call of the sea again. Her seasickness was a distant memory. She tried to convince Tomomi that they would have fantastic adventures if they bought tickets for the cruise ship *Blue Princess*, but Tomomi did not want to leave the island. She said she wanted to return to Fukuoka. Yan realized that their time together was coming to an end, and as a parting present, she gave Tomomi her most treasured possession."

"The pendant."

"Have I already told you this story?"

I shook my head. "Why?"

"You always seem to know when the pendant appears."

"It's not so hard to guess. It's the main thing in the story."

"Is it? I thought it was about finding things and losing things and friends and doing what you believe in."

"It's about all of that, too, but it always comes back to the jewel."

"Indeed," Nanna said. "Now the jewel belonged to Tomomi Taiko, and she cried real tears as she watched her friend sail away on the *Blue Princess*.

"Yan cried, too, but life called her on. She traveled the world for sixteen years altogether and eventually returned to the mountains of Bali where she was born. Frank Feer had been chased from the village many years before, and Yan's father had grown old. Yan nursed him until he died and opened an orphanage in his honor. Yan never had children of her own, but she was mother to hundreds of village children."

"I'm not even going to ask about what happened to Tomomi Taiko."

Nanna just smiled. "You're learning, Ben."

"Learning what?"

"The gentle art of mystery."

"I didn't realize it was an art."

"Oh yes," she said. She kissed my hand and then my cheek. "A fine art."

CHAPTER 10

THROUGH THE GREEN DOOR

Jack sat with Nathan instead of me on Wednesday. They were only one desk over, but they were whispering to each other all day. After lunch, Mr. Jensen started telling us about World War II and how the Japanese were fighting against the Allied Forces. They bombed Pearl Harbor in Hawaii and the American naval base there. They had a reputation as skilled and dangerous soldiers who were ready and willing to die for their country and their cause.

I got to thinking, as Mr. Jensen rambled on, about Tomomi Taiko, and I wondered how the war touched her. Mr. Jensen showed us a map of Japan and the island of Kyushu, where Yan's boat docked. I even found Fukuoka on the map, where Tomomi Taiko lived. I felt sick when

Mr. Jensen spoke about the atomic bombs the Americans dropped on Japan during the war. One landed on Hiroshima. Another landed on Nagasaki, which was on the same small island where Tomomi Taiko lived.

The Americans were bombing their enemies and bringing the war to a close, but they were also bombing my friend. My friend? Well, someone I cared about. Someone whose story was tied together with mine through my Nanna's pendant. I cared about her fate. I didn't want her to die in a nuclear bomb blast.

I met Nathan and Jack at the school gates on my way home that night.

"Want to come over to my place?" Nathan asked. "We're going to play *Green Door* multiplayer."

"I . . . I . . . can't. I have to go home. There's something I need to check."

"Come over after that," Jack said.

"Ok," I said, but I knew I wouldn't. I'd become obsessed with Nanna's story. I wanted to go home and go to bed at four o'clock in the afternoon so she would have to tell me the next chapter. How stupid is that? I love *Green Door*. I'm pretty good, too. Mostly we play *Wizard Watch*. They'd both be destroyed before the afternoon grew dull, that much would be certain. Not literally, of course, just in the game. I love *Green Door*, but the story was drawing me in.

I didn't go to bed at four o'clock. Nanna and Grandpa were in town shopping when I got home, so I jumped on my bike and told Mom I was going to Nathan's house and that I'd be back before dark.

Mom hates war games. She won't let me play any on the computer, and we don't have a games machine in our house, just in case I'm tempted to play a war game. It seems silly when you consider what her dad does for a job.

Besides, war games are *games,* and it all happens on the big plasma screen, and there's no mess to clean up after that war except a few potato chip bags and empty water glasses. Nobody gets hurt, except if you count my legs falling asleep from sitting on the floor of Nathan's living room. *Green Door* was the perfect distraction, and by the time I looked up, it was almost dark.

"Whoops," I said. "Got to go."

"Yeah, good one, Ben," Nathan said. "Quit while you're ahead."

CHAPTER 11

INTO THE PEARLY DEEP

There was something strange going on at home again. Mom and Nanna were clucking with excited laughter when I got home. The silliness continued right through dinner and into the kitchen sink as we washed the dishes. I excused myself, brushed my teeth, and headed to my room to do some math homework. Anything was better than listening to them sniggering at each other in code.

Nanna eventually calmed down. She still had a smile on her face when she came to tuck me in, but it was a sad smile now. One of those smiles you get after laughing yourself sore.

The smile of a tired clown. Nothing was said as she tucked my bedspread too tight. I quietly untucked myself a bit and lay there with my arms by my sides.

Nanna stared straight ahead. I could hear her breathing quietly. For a moment, I thought she was going to tell me what all the fuss was about, but that moment passed, and she picked up where she'd left off.

"Tomomi Taiko rode her bike all the way back to Fukuoka, her heart as heavy as a concrete statue in her chest. Her parents were happy to see her, of course, and she went to work in the market on Monday as if nothing had happened, as if she hadn't ridden across the island and back for all those months. The people at the market realized she was home—to them, she arrived like springtime—and they made a fuss over her, buying her sweets and flowers. One of the children made her an origami lantern out of fine green paper.

"There was one person who noticed more than any of the others—Hayashi Hanamoko. Tomomi and Hayashi had been in school together. Tomomi was the school's best dancer; Hayashi was the school's best swimmer. Hayashi had pulled Tomomi's hair and hidden her pencils. Tomomi had washed her hands after she accidentally touched him and made up skipping songs about all of Hayashi's hair falling out.

"Yes, they were in love, even at school. On that Monday morning at the market, both Tomomi and Hayashi realized they'd changed. They'd grown up, and the love they shared had grown, too. Hayashi didn't pull Tomomi's hair, and when he touched her hand, she didn't want to wash it ever again. She did, of course, but she remembered his touch.

"Months passed and the two fell further in love. After work every day, they would walk to the docks and talk of their future together. The old ladies at the market began whispering about when they would announce their marriage, trying to guess in which season they'd be wed, but it was never to be."

"The war," I said.

"Excuse me?"

"World War II."

"Oh no. This was 1936, and the war was still three years away. No, Hayashi's uncle Kazu Katomita offered him a job working on his lugger."

"What's a lugger?"

"It's a type of sailing boat. This one had a very special purpose. It carried divers specially trained to collect oysters from the ocean floor."

"Hayashi was a very good swimmer," I remembered.

"Yes, indeed he was. The best his school had to offer. Diving for oysters didn't sound like an exciting job, but Kazu explained that inside each oyster was a pearl, and the pearls would make them all very wealthy. Hayashi could use his natural skill in the water and get rich at the same time.

"The only catch was that there were very few oysters left in the sea surrounding Japan, so they had to go a long way from home to find them. A long, long way from home. Hayashi would come home rich, but he'd be away for more than a year. Hayashi was torn. He wanted the job on the lugger, but he didn't want to leave Tomomi. When they sat and talked about it, they both cried. They understood each other, and when Hayashi Hanamoko asked Tomomi Taiko if she would wait for him, Tomomi said yes. She said she'd wait as long as it took for Hayashi to find the wealth and adventure he was looking for. When Kazu's lugger was loaded and they were ready to leave, Tomomi gave him . . ."

"The pendant. This sounds like Angelina Angel and Samuel Stetson and World War I all over again."

"No, she didn't give him the pendant, and the war was only whispers in 1936. She gave him an ornate wooden box lined inside with blood red silk. It contained a bottle of ink and a small calligraphy brush. It was a writing set so that Hayashi could send letters to Tomomi from the ports they visited and tell of his adventures. So they could stay in contact. Hayashi promised to write, and they parted in a flood of tears and more heart-wrenching farewells.

"Six months passed, and every day, Tomomi would stop the postman, and every day the postman's response was the same. 'Sorry, Tomomi, nothing for you today.' Poor Tomomi had many sleepless nights thinking that Hayashi had already forgotten her or, worse, been lost at sea.

"On the two hundred twenty-second day after his departure, a letter finally arrived. Did I say letter? It was more like a novel. Hayashi had written something every day. Sometimes he had written twice a day, but they had never gone ashore to mail his letters until then. Tomomi vanished into her room and didn't stop reading for one whole day and one whole night. She didn't eat and didn't sleep for that entire time."

"What about the bathroom?" I asked.

"Well, she went to the bathroom, obviously, but she took the letter she was reading with her."

"I see," I said.

"The story she read was a bold adventure full of mysterious sea creatures, feats of survival, big winds, and wild oceans. The bundle of letters had come all the way from Broome in Western Australia, where Uncle Kazu had finally found the bountiful oyster beds he'd dreamed about as a boy. They slept some nights ashore now and had an entire week when a hurricane rolled along the coast and they were forced to stay in the port.

"Some boats went out while the weather was still unpredictable and never returned. On their own boat, two divers had died, both taken by sharks while they worked. It was a hard and dangerous job, there was no point in denying that, but Hayashi was earning good money and had little need or desire to spend it. There were many Japanese people living in Broome, mostly working with pearls, and Hayashi made lots of friends. He was learning English from an Australian schoolboy, and he was teaching the boy Japanese in exchange.

"In short, things were going as planned. Hayashi wrote that he loved Tomomi. He hoped she would wait for him and that, as soon as he returned, he would ask her father's permission to marry her.

"After reading Hayashi's letters for a whole day and night, Tomomi danced. She danced all the way to work and home again. She danced while helping to prepare meals, and she danced in the *onsen* (hot springs) until one of the old ladies told her to stop. She was just so happy. With his letter to read, it didn't feel as if Hayashi was half a world away, and she knew that, one day, they'd be together."

Nanna rubbed at her eyes. She'd been crying, and I hadn't noticed. This chapter wasn't like Angelina Angel and Samuel Stetson at all. This was the way Nanna and Grandpa lived their lives: half a world apart and knowing that one day they'd be together.

I took Nanna's hand, and she smiled down at me.

"I'm a silly old fool," she said. "This part gets me every time."

I wanted to say that I knew why it got to her. I wanted to tell her that the story of Hayashi and Tomomi was just like the story of her own life, but I didn't say a thing. I just held her hand and did the best listening I'd ever done. Mr. Jensen would have been proud of me. I didn't miss a word, and I didn't miss a word *between* the words either. What good is a good story if it doesn't have a good listener?

"There was a return address on Hayashi's letter, written in the strange, squiggly letters of English. Tomomi copied it perfectly and wrote to Hayashi whenever time permitted. It was a long-distance love affair, and their love for each other and their dedication grew stronger as the months passed.

"The months kept on passing, though, until they became a year. Uncle Kazu was still making money and had no intention of sailing back to Japan. Hayashi worked hard and saved even harder, but his heart ached for Tomomi. He wanted to come home, but he was Kazu's best diver, and if he left, Kazu would not find another diver strong enough to replace him.

"A year became two years. Hayashi and Tomomi wrote back and forth. They wrote about what they did during the day, and they wrote of how dreamy their life together would be after the work was done. Kazu gave Hayashi a beautiful, perfect pearl . . . one that Hayashi himself had collected. Hayashi had it made into a necklace and mailed it to Tomomi.

"Tomomi loved that gift more than anything she had ever received—even more than the pendant her beautiful friend Yan had given her. She couldn't wear the pearl and the dark jewel together, and once she realized this, she packed up the pendant and sent it off to Hayashi in Australia. The jewel's beauty brought tears to his eyes . . . that and the fact that his beloved Tomomi was thousands of miles away and this dark stone would remind him of that every time he looked at it."

"That sounds like some sort of cruel torture," I said.

"Yes, in a way it did rub salt into his wounded heart, but in time the pendant came to represent the life they would share together *after* the pain of being apart."

Nanna sighed.

"And?" I said.

"I wish life were that simple."

"Why? What happened?"

"Another year passed. War broke out in Europe and spread to the rest of the world. Countries were called upon to choose sides, and the Japanese tied their fate to Italy and Germany. Some say they were victims of circumstance, but the fact remains that they became the enemy of the Australians, and as such, the Australians were told by their government to be suspicious of people of Japanese descent who lived among them.

"They created internment camps where they put anybody who looked Japanese or Italian or German. The government made them lock up their friends. Some of the people they rounded up had been born in Australia and had lived their entire lives there. Those who weren't locked up went off to join the war effort. The pearl industry had no workers.

"Internment camps were prisons, work camps, but the people of Broome took care of their friends. Hayashi and Kazu and most of the pearlers in the west of Australia were locked up in Broome. The wardens were strict about the government's decision that prisoners weren't allowed to send or receive mail, and for months there was no communication. Three months' worth of letters were returned to Tomomi unopened. She felt her world crumbling.

"Help came in the form of English lessons. The Australian schoolboy visited Hayashi in the internment camp to continue his Japanese lessons and to teach his friend English. Hayashi spoke to the boy about not being able to get messages to his beloved Tomomi, and the boy offered to be their go-between. Hayashi wrote a letter, and the boy sent it off for him.

"A reply came three weeks later, sent straight to the boy's house, and he smuggled it into the internment camp on his next visit. For three whole years, the boy visited once a week, without fail. Others wrote letters, and the boy mailed them. By the time Hayashi and the other interns were released, the boy was a fine young man. Hayashi owed him so much. They all did. He tried to give the young man money, but he wouldn't accept it. Kazu offered him pearls, but there was no way he was going to accept them either.

"After the war, Tomomi could wait no longer. Carrying a single suitcase, she boarded a cruise ship bound for Australia. The only problem was that she would be docking in Sydney, and Hayashi was working with his uncle on the other side of the country. The pearl industry was just getting on its feet again after the war, and there was no time to lose.

"It was the young man who saved the day again. He drove a military jeep all the way from Broome to Sydney and back again with special cargo."

"Tomomi?"

"Yes, and her suitcase. They chatted in broken Japanese and English as they drove across the country towards Broome, slept on the ground, and ate whatever the young man could shoot with his rifle. Soon Tomomi found a rhythm in the journey. They would rise before the sun and drive all day. The young man taught Tomomi how to operate the car, and they shared the driving. Tomomi was behind the wheel when they crashed."

I drew a shocked breath. I didn't mean to, but I'd thought I knew how this part of the story would end, and it twisted right there in front of me. "Were they ok?"

"Oh yes, they were fine. The jeep's radiator was broken, which was a problem, but everything else was ok.

"It took a day for the young man to repair the radiator using mud and sap and one of Tomomi's fine silk kimonos. Four more days of driving lay ahead of them, and they were both tired. The repairs to the jeep were good, but they had to stop every two hours and top off the water in the radiator. The radiator drank more water than they did.

"On the last day, as they drove through the desert towards Broome, they ran out of water. The radiator dried up, and the engine broke."

"Could he fix it?"

Nanna shook her head. "Not a chance. Their only option was to walk the last sixty miles through the desert."

"With no water?"

"No water," Nanna said. She rubbed her eyes. "They almost made it, too."

"You mean they died out there?"

"Oh, goodness no. They walked for a couple of hours, and then a passing truck picked them up and drove them right into town."

I sighed with relief.

"You can imagine the festivities when Hayashi and Tomomi finally met up again after all those years. They were married on the beach in Broome, and the young man and Kazu were the best men. Two of the local women attended the bride, and the captain of one of the other luggers married the couple.

"Hayashi and Tomomi lived long and productive lives. They had five children— three girls and two boys. They're buried in the cemetery in Broome. You can still see their headstones etched in Japanese."

"What about the pendant?"

"What about it?"

"Where did it end up?"

Nanna leaned in and kissed my cheek.

"Oh no you don't. That's not the end."

She smiled. "Hayashi gave the pendant to the young man for all the love and kindness he had showed them, and to his delight, the young man accepted the gift."

"That's it?"

"Goodnight, Ben."

"Who was the young man?"

"Goodnight, Ben."

"Grrrrr!"

CHAPTER 12
THE OLD LADY DIES

We all went to a movie on Thursday night, as we usually did. Grandpa wanted to see the war movie we'd seen the week before, but we convinced him to see the one about a diamond robbery. I think that was the one Mom wanted to see anyway.

The diamond robbery had everything I like in movies—action, action and more action. Well, that's not strictly true, because I've been bored by action movies with no story behind the cars blowing up and the buildings falling down. I like to laugh, too. Just once or twice. Or three hundred times. Ok, I like a little bit of romance, too. The heroes have to win, and the girl has to get the guy or the guy has to get the girl.

I sat next to Grandpa and he tried to cover my ears when the characters used bad language. Then he tried to cover my eyes during the romance part. He was too busy watching the movie to realize I could see under his fingers.

The heroes in the diamond robbery movie were the bad guys—the thieves—but even though I thought they were clever and super cool, I didn't want to go outside after the movie and rob the first bank I saw. I'll leave that to the experts.

"Broome was a ghost town after the war. Most of the pearlers moved on, but Kazu and his crew stayed. Hayashi's friend, the young man, couldn't find any work, and he said his farewells and made the long journey south to the city of Fremantle, where he found a job in a funeral parlor."

"What? Burying dead people?"

Nanna nodded. "Somebody had to do it, and he was very good at his job. He wore the pendant under his suit until one day he stopped to help a woman struggling with her umbrella. Fremantle's beaches face the Indian Ocean, and sometimes the winds roar into the town and rattle the houses. The young man helped the woman tame her unruly umbrella, but in doing so, the chain holding the pendant broke. He didn't feel it slide from his neck and land in the gutter. He lost a precious thing that day, but he found something more precious than the stone."

I couldn't think of a single thing more precious than the stone, with all its beauty and its value and the memories it held. I looked at Nanna, puzzled.

"Love. He helped the woman with her umbrella, and the woman asked him if she could repay him by buying him a coffee. Well, the man said yes, and the rest, they say, is history."

"What? No way. That can't be the end."

"No, of course not. They got married, and one year later, they got divorced, but they were still friends."

"That's a stupid story," I grumbled.

Nanna shrugged. "Perhaps. Not every tale has a happy ending. We've discussed that."

"What about the pendant?"

"Well, the man was so taken by the woman with the umbrella, he didn't notice that it was missing until the next morning. He searched everywhere for it, but a storm had rolled in off the Indian Ocean during the night and washed the streets clean. It washed the pendant away."

"That can't be the end. That's as dumb as getting married and then divorced."

Nanna grinned. It was a cruel grin. She knew I was addicted to the story, and she was teasing me with it, I knew it.

She got up to leave, and I grabbed the pocket of her dress and tugged until she huffed and sat down again.

"For many years, the pendant lay in the muck and sand at the bottom of the drain. Storm after storm washed it closer to the sea, until the flood of 1953 flushed it out of the city. It may never have been found again if it weren't for the careful eye of Matilda Murchison. She was an old woman then. She lived three streets away from the beach, and she took her dogs—Patsy and Flipper—for a walk along the sand every morning, come rain, wind, hail or shine.

"Matilda Murchison collected things. Every spare space in her house was covered with shells and knick-knacks she found washed up, and she had a sharp eye for bits of treasure. On the edge of the raging outflow from the storm drain, she spotted a flash of gold. Just one tiny link stuck out from the muck. She bent to collect that fleck of gold and realized she'd found a chain. Looped on the chain was a solid gold setting which held in place the most beautiful dark jewel she'd ever seen.

"Carefully, she dipped the prize in the water, and it was flushed instantly clean. It seemed to glow in the morning light. She looked along the beach, but there was nobody around. Nobody to claim the pendant. She thought briefly about handing the jewel to the police, but in the end she thought it was too lovely to part with. She felt that way about lots of things, that's why her house was so full of stuff. She already wore a necklace . . . glass beads on a fake gold chain . . . and she took that one off and called the pendant her own.

"Matilda Murchison treasured that pendant. She wore it from that day to her last, and she didn't show it to anybody."

"Nobody?"

Nanna shook her head. "Not a soul. She was frightened that the original owner might spot it and take it from her. It had happened with many of those who owned the jewel—Matilda Murchison fell in love with the thing, and it became her most prized possession.

"Love does strange things to people. So does hate. Matilda had two sons, Michael and Murray. Michael loved his mother dearly and wanted nothing but the best for her. He worked as a lawyer in Perth, and he brought his mother little gifts every time he came to visit. Murray, on the other hand, did not get along with his mother. Not at all. He was a lawyer, too, also working in Perth, but no two brothers could be more different. Murray couldn't bear to be in the same room with Matilda, and he had been that way since he was a child.

"Anyway, Matilda Murchison became ill. Michael feared that the doctors were right, that it was only a matter of time before she slipped off her perch, so to speak."

"Slipped off her perch? That's horrible. She wasn't a canary."

"No. She was definitely not a canary. It's an old saying. Sorry, Ben. Anyway, where was I? Ah yes, Michael feared that Matilda would pass away without his brother having said goodbye, so he arranged for Murray to visit her in the hospital. Murray said that he didn't want to go, but Michael insisted. In the end, Murray went to his mother and sat at her bedside. They were quiet for a long time, and then Murray took his mother's hand and held it. He apologized for being such a horrible child and an even more horrible man.

"Hearing this made Matilda Murchison cry, and Murray cried, too. Matilda said that he wasn't a horrible child and that she was very proud of his success as a man. She apologized for being such a hard mother as he was growing up. Later that night, after Murray had said his final goodbyes, Matilda died. Naturally, the men cried, but life still had twists of fate to offer.

"Michael and Murray shared the burden of dressing their mother for her burial. They discovered the jewel together. It was obviously worth a lot of money. Murray wanted to keep it. Michael said that, if it were his choice alone, he'd bury it with their mother, but he trusted his brother with the decision. Murray held the jewel and stared at it for a long time. Should he take it or leave it?"

Nanna stared at me. "Well?"

"Well what?"

"Should he take it or leave it?"

My head was spinning. He could take it and sell it. The money would be nice, though he didn't really need it. He could leave it around her neck, and she could wear it right to the very end. That would be considerate. He could take it and wear it and be reminded of his mother every time he looked at it. Being reminded of her might be good or bad or both.

"I think he should leave it. It was hers. He has no need for it. There must be other ways to remember her."

Nanna bowed her head. "Indeed." She kissed my forehead.

"That's it?"

"For tonight."

"But the story isn't finished yet."

"It never will be."

"No, I mean, this little bit of the story hasn't ended."

"Oh, it's an ending all right. In the trade it's known as a 'cliff-hanger.'"

"That's not very fair!"

"Not much of a cliff-hanger either," said Nanna with a chuckle.

"Well, no. The jewel obviously isn't buried in a Perth cemetery, is it?"

Nanna held her pendant. "Not now, no."

"What, so you're a grave robber now?"

"Worse things happen at sea, you know."

"Arghh!"

I suppose it was a better ending than, 'That, my dear, is another story,' though it wasn't much different.

As luck would have it, I made it to school early on Friday. Jack and Nathan hadn't even arrived. It was the first time I'd beaten them to school all year, and I made sure they knew it.

"Where have you guys been? I've been waiting for hours."

"It's good you're here early for once," Jack said.

Nathan put his hand on my shoulder. "We have a proposition," he whispered.

"What sort of proposition?" I asked, warily.

"We need to borrow your monkey."

"Your inner monkey," Jack explained. "We want you to climb for us."

"Be, like, our man servant," Nathan added.

"Your slave?"

"No, not slave," Jack said. "Professional climber. The guy who keeps the supplies coming up to the adventurers."

"Yes," Nathan said. "You wouldn't have to sleep up in the tree."

"There isn't room," I pointed out.

"True," Nathan agreed. "Even if there were, all you'd have to do is bring stuff up to us."

"Be our supply man. Our climber," Jack said. He cupped a hand over my ear and whispered, "I think it would be more fun if you were there."

I smiled at that. I could have all the fun of the sleepover without the dangers of sleeping on a rickety platform at a high altitude. "Where do I sleep?"

"We could set up my camping tent," Nathan suggested. "There's an inflatable mattress and sleeping bag and everything."

"Ok," I said, before I'd thought it through.

Jack grinned.

Nathan slapped my back. "You won't regret this."

I already was, though. Nanna's story! We were getting so close to the end, I could feel it.

I stressed about it until lunchtime, and then one sensible thought made it through the fretting— it wasn't like watching a series on TV. Nanna was hardly going to tell the story without me. Besides, I wasn't even sure that Mom would let me sleep over at Nathan's.

When Mom called Nathan's mom that afternoon to see if it was ok to sleep over, she explained that we were planning to sleep in the treehouse.

"Are you sure it's safe?" Mom asked me later.

"No, I'm not sure," I said. "I'll be sleeping in a tent on the ground."

Mom patted my head. "Very wise."

I found Nanna in her room before I left. She had all of her socks out on the bed. There must have been close to fifty pairs.

"Are they all yours?"

Nanna looked embarrassed. "Mostly mine. Some used to belong to your mother, and these . . ." she said, tossing me a pair, "are almost certainly yours."

"Are you sure?" I asked. "All the cool nannas are wearing spider socks these days."

Nanna chuckled. "Indeed."

"I'm going to a friend's place for a sleepover tonight. We'll have to continue the story tomorrow night."

"Yes, of course," Nanna said. She stopped her sorting and looked straight at me.

"What?"

"It's just . . ."

"Yes?"

She ran her pendant from side to side along its chain. "We're almost at the end."

"Really?"

She nodded, looking at the scattered socks.

"Some ends are just beginnings in disguise," I said.

She smiled at that. "So true."

We hugged, and she kissed my cheek.

"Have fun."

"I will."

Then, as I was leaving, she grabbed my sleeve.

"What?" I asked.

Her mouth opened and closed, and then she smiled. "It's nothing," she said.

"What?" I insisted.

"It doesn't matter. You have your sleepover, and we'll catch up tomorrow."

I stood there for a long time. Nanna smoothed my shirt where she'd grabbed me. "Have fun," she said again.

I stared. She just grinned.

She had nearly told me. That matter of national security, that secret decision she'd had to make was hanging there behind her lips. I could almost hear her thinking it. I wanted to get on my knees and pull at her dress like a little kid, pleading and crying until she told me, but another part of me knew how to live with untold secrets, knew how to let her tell me on her own time. In her own words.

"Tomorrow?" I said.

"Yes, tomorrow."

I kissed her cheek.

It was a date.

It took us half an hour to set up the tent. It wouldn't fit right under the tree, so we set it up on the lawn nearby. Close enough that I could hear them calling me if they got altitude sickness.

When the sun finally went down, the darkness settled around us like a blanket—a blanket we'd pulled over our heads. The only light that made it into the yard came from the neighbor's back porch, and apparently it didn't make it up into the treehouse.

"Ben!" Nathan hollered.

I'd just gotten into my sleeping bag. "What?"

"We need a light."

"You have a light," I said.

"The batteries are dead."

I turned on my own. "You can't have mine. I need mine."

"Get some new batteries from my mom."

Nathan's mom was on the computer. I asked for batteries, and her eyebrows climbed up her forehead in surprise. She looked at her watch.

"Those batteries didn't last very long," she said. "Still, it won't be long before the three of you will be sleeping in the living room, I'll bet."

She said it like a challenge, as if she wanted to have a real bet about whether we would stay outside the whole night.

Anyway, after rummaging in the drawer beside the computer, she handed me a new package of batteries.

"How much do you want to bet?" I asked.

Nathan's mom laughed. "Are you serious? You think you'll stay out all night?"

"How much?"

She pinched her chin in thought, and then a smile twitched up the corners of her mouth. "I'll tell you what," she said. "Stay out all night, and I'll cook as many pancakes as you can eat for breakfast."

I licked my lips. "And if we fail?"

"The three of you have to clean my car, inside and out."

I held out my hand, and she shook it.

We lost the bet. About twenty minutes after I delivered the batteries and told them about the challenge, it started raining. I could hear it drumming on the tent. I heard muttering and commotion, and then I heard an almighty crack, followed by a chorus of sickening squeals and breaking branches.

The next thing I heard was Nathan screaming. His mom was at the scene before I'd untangled myself from the sleeping bag.

Nathan's arm was broken.

His mom was a nurse, and she knew about those things, but you didn't have to be a nurse to figure it out—his arm bent where it shouldn't bend. Nathan's mom took him to the hospital, and Jack, who had a scratch on his cheek, and I camped in their living room.

After Nathan and his mom had gone and Nathan's dad had made sure we were comfortable, Jack and I started laughing. We started and we couldn't stop. We weren't laughing about Nathan's broken arm. We were laughing about the fact that we'd survived. Who needed to travel to Japan, Indonesia, or Broome to have an adventure?

When Nathan's mom got back from the hospital with Nathan, she said we didn't have to clean her car the next morning, but I told her that a bet was a bet. Jack and I did the work while Nathan pointed out parts that we'd missed, his plastered arm in a sling across his chest. Sometimes, even when you lose you win.

CHAPTER 14
A CRUEL CONUNDRUM

Nanna and Grandad didn't get home until late the next night. Off engaged in mysterious matters of national security was my guess. I was already in bed. They came in to kiss me goodnight, but only Nanna stayed.

I had my own story to tell that night. Nanna was a good listener, covering her mouth in shock when Nathan broke his arm and laughing out loud when Nathan's mom made us pancakes anyway.

She patted my hand. "You're a good storyteller, Ben. It runs in the family, and I'm very proud of you."

"Thanks. I learned from the best."

She smiled, but she was looking at the floor between her feet. A cloud of sadness hung over her.

"What is it?" I asked.

She shook her head. "There's one more chapter to tell you."

I snuggled under the covers. That was as good as a promise. One more chapter, and then she'd tell me what was bugging her.

"As luck would have it," she began, "the funeral director in charge of Matilda Murchison's burial was none other than the Japanese-speaking man from Broome."

"The one who drove Tomomi from Sydney?"

Nanna nodded.

"Married and divorced?"

"Yes, and married again. To the same woman!"

My mouth hung open in disbelief.

"One month after their divorce became final, they met on the street as they had done the very first time they'd met and realized they were both still as much in love as they'd been back then. Their friends thought they were crazy, but they all came to their second wedding anyway, and this time they got it right. In no time at all, they'd started a family, and the man's business at the funeral parlor boomed."

Nanna stopped speaking and stared at me. "He couldn't believe his eyes when the body of Matilda Murchison arrived in his office wearing the pendant he'd lost—wearing the jewel he'd been given by his Japanese friends in Broome. It *had* to be the same one. Now he was faced with a cruel conundrum."

"Conundrum?"

"A puzzle. A challenge."

I decided to rise to the challenge, and Nanna nodded as I thought out loud: "It was his pendant, but now it belonged to the dead woman. She was dead, so she wouldn't need it anymore, but even I know it's pretty sick to steal from dead people. Still, who's going to know?"

"Precisely," Nanna said. "The man was tempted. He knew that he'd be the last one to see her in her coffin before the lid closed forever. He'd have the time, the motive, and the opportunity to take the dark stone back."

I thought about the conundrum some more. What would I have done in the same situation? Why didn't this character in the very last chapter have a name? It was then that it dawned on me.

I knew who he was.

"I would have spoken to Matilda's sons. I would have explained the situation. I would have left the decision in their hands."

"That's exactly what the man did," Nanna continued. "He made Matilda Murchison as beautiful as she could be. It was his best work ever, and before the ceremony actually began, he took the brothers aside and told them the story. He told the story with such passion and conviction that the brothers believed him. They realized that their mother had probably found the jewel and that it probably *had* originally belonged to the funeral director."

"So they gave him the pendant?"

"No," Nanna said. "Not at first. The brothers argued. Murray thought that, if the pendant wasn't going into their mother's grave, then *he* should have it. Michael thought that, if his mother were alive, she'd give the pendant to the rightful owner.

"The ceremony went on as planned. There were many mourners saying their last farewells because Matilda Murchison was a familiar presence to the people of Fremantle. She'd been beachcombing for years, and everybody knew her. As the funeral director lowered the lid on Matilda's coffin for the last time, he tried not to look at the pendant. He tried hard, but he still noticed a flash of gold around her neck. He swallowed hard as he clipped the lid shut. He'd done the right thing."

"No!" I said, pulling my own hair. "It was his!"

Nanna held up a finger. I shoved my head back into my pillow in frustration.

"It *was* his. After the funeral, the Murchison brothers held a wake at the Esplanade hotel. Matilda's friends and family got together to celebrate her life. The funeral director made an appearance after his work was done, and people shook his hand and told him how lovely the service had been. Michael Murchison shook his hand, too. He shook his hand and pressed something into his palm. Something smooth and heavy."

"The pendant? How . . . I thought . . ."

"Yes, the pendant. While nobody was watching, Michael swapped the pendant for a necklace his mother had always loved. Glass beads on an imitation gold chain. He'd made it for her himself when he was a young man, and his mother had worn it for many years."

"She took it off," I said. "She took it off when she found the pendant."

"True," Nanna said. "She wore it to her grave instead of the pendant now in the hands of the funeral director."

"How come you never mentioned his name?"

"Who?"

"The funeral director."

Nanna smiled. "Because you would have recognized him."

"Recognized him? How?"

"The funeral director was my father. The beautiful woman with the umbrella—the woman he married, divorced, and then married again—was my mother. Your great-grandmother Elise."

"I knew it!"

Nanna's whole face glowed with a smile.

"Your father gave it to your mother who gave it to you."

"More or less."

Nanna reached behind her neck and unclasped the chain. She held the beautiful jewel and stared at it for a moment.

"My father realized that the stone was lucky, but only when given in love. He gave it to his wife on her birthday. Given with love, received with love. She gave it to me on my twenty-first birthday, but we knew it better by then. The beautiful jewel was not lucky or unlucky. It was not influenced by the giver or the receiver. There was no karma or magic, it just made whatever thoughts you had stronger. If you were grasping and greedy, then more of that came your way. If you were generous and kind, then more of *that* appeared in your life."

I suddenly had a sense of the jewel. The stories Nanna had told all whispered about its power.

"Sit up," Nanna commanded.

I did as I was told. My heart raced as she hung the pendant around my neck. I couldn't breathe properly. With the chain fastened, I finally realized how heavy and serious the piece of jewelry really was.

"No," I said. "I don't deserve it. I'm not old enough for the responsibility. I . . ."

"Oh, you're old enough," Nanna said.

"How do you know?"

"I just know. Call it intuition."

"Why now? Why me?"

"Well, I discussed it with your mother, and she thought it would be something to remember me by. I won't be around forever."

Nanna looked straight at me. I could see tears welling in her eyes, and the sight of that made my own eyes flood.

"Remember you? I knew it! You're sick. You're going to die. I *knew* it."

Nanna laughed hard with her head tilted back. "Good grief, no, Ben. Whatever gave you that idea?"

"All the whispering and secrets in the house. All the conversations that ended as soon as I entered the room."

She chuckled and then sat on the side of my bed and held my chin with both hands. She looked straight into my eyes. "I'm not dying, Ben. I'm not even sick. Fit as a fiddle."

"Then what . . ."

"Your grandfather has asked me to come and live with him overseas."

I swallowed. I felt sad, but relieved.

"I said yes," she went on. "It's all top secret, of course, but we're leaving on Monday."

"Tomorrow? *This* Monday?"

She nodded.

I sat there in bed, totally stunned for a good minute. Tears trickled down onto my cheeks, and I rubbed them away with my pajama sleeve. I didn't want the pendant, I wanted Nanna. I wanted Grandpa. I didn't want the responsibility of the jewel.

"Why do I get this?" I asked, holding the chain, frightened even to touch the sacred stone. "Why didn't you give it to Mom?"

Nanna shrugged. "It wasn't meant for her. It was meant for you."

"I'm just a kid."

"Exactly."

"I'm not ready for the responsibility."

"Oh, I think you are. It's not supposed to be a burden."

"What if I lose it?"

Nanna shrugged again. "It's been lost before."

"What if I *really* lose it? Break it?"

She patted my shoulder. "It *really* doesn't matter. It will move on when the time is right."

"What if . . . deep down . . . I'm evil and the stone makes me more evil?"

Nanna did another head-back laugh that made me want to shout. I was serious!

"I don't think you're in any danger of becoming an evil monster, Ben," she said softly. "All you have to do is be kind to yourself and watch your thoughts."

"But . . ."

"Can you take care of it?" Nanna asked, suddenly serious.

I cradled the stone in my palm and looked at it, really looked at it, for the first time. It was still warm from Nanna's skin. It was almost black, but when I stared into that dark pool, I saw colors—flashes in every rainbow shade. I fell in love, as so many before me had done. I finally knew what all the fuss was about. I could see why it had been bought and sold for such huge sums of money. It didn't belong around my neck—it belonged in a museum somewhere.

I unclasped it and handed it back to Nanna, but she wouldn't take it.

"It's yours," she whispered.

I screwed up my face.

"There's a secret you need to know."

"I'm not sure if I want to be part of any secret."

"It's important. Even your mother doesn't know about it."

I dangled the pendant in front of her face.

"Look on the back," she whispered.

"What?"

"Read the inscription."

I turned the thing in my hand and read the small writing.

It can't be, I thought. My head reeled. It just wasn't possible.

"Can you read it?"

"Of course," I breathed.

"What does it say?" Nanna said and leaned close so I could whisper back.

"It says, 'Made in China.'"

She smiled.

"It wasn't found in the desert?"

She stared.

"It wasn't fashioned by a city jeweler?"

She blinked.

"It wasn't ever a brooch?"

If you ever needed a picture of a face to put in your dictionary next to the definition of "confused," that was the moment to snap a shot of me. I didn't want Nanna to leave. I didn't want the stories to stop, but I'd also discovered that the stories she'd been telling— all the stories—had been exactly that: stories.

"What about Billy Bobby Burton, the man who found the stone? He was real, wasn't he?"

"Of course," Nanna said. "He had a memorable name, and I remembered him from my childhood. Such a beautiful piano player."

"He didn't find the stone?"

Nanna smiled a cheeky smile, and I had to laugh. I had to laugh out loud because I had been tricked. She'd sucked me in. She'd got me hook, line, and sinker, reeled me in, put me on a plate, and gobbled me all up.

"You lied to me!" I moaned.

"In a manner of speaking, yes. Every story is a lie. Even the ones you read in the newspaper that are supposed to be real are only an approximation of the truth."

"I won't believe another thing you say ever again! Ever!" I wailed.

"Good," Nanna said.

"Good?"

"Yes, it's healthy to be a bit suspicious."

"Don't trust anybody?"

"It's not about trusting them or not trusting them. It's about the nature of truth."

"What's that supposed to mean?"

"Even the biggest liar can teach you a truth about lying."

"Now that sounds like a riddle."

"Let me put it this way . . . When we go shopping, we don't take one of everything off the shelf."

"Sometimes Mom gets close."

Nanna snorted. "True, but we really only come out with what we need."

"So?"

"So stories are the same. We need to pick through what the storyteller is offering us and find the things that mean something. The treasures. The jewels. The things that feel like truth to us."

Put like that, Nanna's lies didn't seem so cruel. Hearing Nanna's stories wasn't supposed to be like reading the newspaper; it was more like watching cartoons, playing *Green Door*, or going to a movie. Entertainment first.

"Is there really a monkey forest in Bali?"

"Yes."

"Pearl divers in Broome?"

"Even to this day."

"Some parts are true. Some are lies."

Nanna leaned close. "Details," she whispered. "The details make the stories believable."

"Have you been to Broome?"

She smiled. "Yes I have. And Fukuoka and France and Belgium and Germany, but not during the war."

It clicked together in my head. Nanna and Grandpa had been to all the places in the stories. Grandpa's work took him around the world, and Mom and Nanna had traveled with him for years and years before I was born. Nanna had been collecting details all her life.

I held that one consistent detail, the one from every story, in my fingers and shifted it in the light. "Where did you get this?"

"My father gave it to my mother shortly before she died."

"It's beautiful."

"It certainly is."

"I can't keep it," I said.

"Please," Nanna said. "I'm not saying you have to wear it."

I knew I would keep it, treasure it, maybe even wear it from time to time.

"I'm going to miss you," I said.

Nanna hugged me. I could feel her tears hot on my own cheek. "I'll miss you, too."

EPILOGUE

I had the day off from school on Monday. Dad went to work. I wore the pendant under my shirt. We piled into Mom's station wagon with my grandparents' luggage, and Grandpa insisted on driving. He's not really a good passenger, or so he says. He took us to the international terminal parking lot, and I wheeled the cart with the suitcases on it all the way to the check-in desk.

Through security.

I held my breath as I walked through the metal detectors. The machine beeped, and everybody looked. I got so red that I thought my face would actually start bleeding.

"Anything metallic in your pockets?" the security guard asked. He ushered me back through the detectors and they beeped again.

"The pendant," Nanna whispered.

"The sign said gold was ok," I said.

Nanna huffed a breathy laugh. "I don't think it's actually gold."

I drew the pendant from beneath my shirt, and the guard whistled. "Fine piece of jewelry," he said.

I looped it off my neck, and another guard put it in a plastic box and fed it through the x-ray machine. I held my breath and walked back through the metal detector. No beeping.

Grandpa bought us burgers for lunch, but I couldn't finish mine. My guts were all wobbly on the inside.

Nanna grabbed my hand across the table. She looked like a sad puppy. I poked my bottom lip out, and she squeezed my fingers.

I cried when they disappeared down the corridor and onto their plane. I mean, it wasn't like they were dying or anything, and I knew I'd see them again, but they were a chapter I didn't want to finish. Ever. Their story—my story—would go on. We were two pieces of string stretching off in different directions that would eventually knit back together again. Hey . . . that was pretty good! Perhaps Nanna was right? Maybe I had inherited the storyteller gene?

"Where were you yesterday?" Nathan asked when I got to school on Tuesday morning.

"Airport," I said. "Saying goodbye to my Nanna and Grandpa."

"What's that around your neck?" Jack asked.

I pulled the pendant out of my school shirt, and Nathan and Jack both gasped.

"Where did you get that?" Nathan asked.

"From my Nanna."

"Very cool," Jack said.

"It started life in a mine in the desert. A man with the unfortunate but memorable name of Billy Bobby Burton found it around the turn of the last century, but he never actually saw the stone in the daylight. He was struck blind by a falling rock as he wedged out the jewel from the hard earth."

"Seriously?" Nathan asked.

Jack sat down and crossed his legs in front of him on the playground, like a little kid. "Tell us more," he said.

Just then, the bell rang.

"How did it get here if he was blind?" Nathan asked.

"That, my friends, is another story," I said.

They both moaned.

I kept my lips in a straight, firm line, but inside I was smiling like the sun peeking out from behind gray clouds. Another story indeed.